Nola goes to the Zoo

Written by Kimmie Tubre and T.J. Barnes

Illustrated by Mark A. Druhet

The Nola Louise Project

Text ©2013 by Kimmie Tubre and T.J. Barnes

Published in the United States of America

ISBM 978-0615784786

For Sarah with love!

There once was a curious little girl, with baby doll shoes and fluffy curls. Her eyes were brown and wide to the world. Nola Louise was her name.

Today was her day, she thought. I want to have fun and play. "What should I do today?"

Nola opened her window with a yawn to see the brand new day. "Oh how lovely it is outside! What shall I do?" she'd say. With a smile on her face and a gleam in her eyes, she thought, I know what I could do. "I should do something to enjoy this lovely day. I'll ask to go to the zoo."

Down in the south is a zoo like none other, with animals galore.
So much fun, so much to do!
So much that Nola could explore.

She thought about it over and over again, getting excited from minute to minute.

With a smile on her face, she ran down the stairs yelling, "Mommy, mommy, we must go to the zoo!.

The one down in Audubon, I hear there's lots to do. All kinds of things to see, and animals galore. Oh mommy, please can we go? I just want to explore."

Nola's mommy smiled wide as could be and said,
"I'd like to explore too.
But before we go to the zoo, I have some chores to do."

Nola was so happy. She said, "Mommy I can help you finish."

They both cleaned the house from top to bottom,
And from the left side to the right.
She really wanted to go to the zoo, and stay until the night.

Her mom was very pleased Nola helped with all the chores.
She wiped down all the tables, even helped to sweep the floors.

Mommy smiled with joy and said,
"Now that you have done the chores, we can head out to the zoo.
The one down in Audubon with so much for you to do.
They're many things for us to see, and animals galore.

Crocodiles and elephants and much more to explore.
I'd like to see a lion, maybe a monkey or two.
I can't wait to get there either. I'd like to explore with you."

So they hopped on their bikes and rode down to the zoo.
You know the one in Audubon with so much for them to do.
They saw large tigers, monkeys, and goats. They even saw a bat.
They saw some snakes and lizards, and a nutria rat.

Nola was excited about the animals.
She smiled from ear to ear.
Her mom smiled back then asked, "What's that I hear?"

A large chirp could be heard from one side to the next.
There was a large aviary with birds that flew from net to net.
Inside they saw a toucan, a parrot, and one blue-jay.
The birds made lots of noise; they had a lot to say.

Butterflies fluttered over a pond and Nola looked down to see the fish.
They move their fins about and splashed the water, "swish swish"

Nola left the aviary and smiled from ear to ear.
"Did you love the zoo?" asked mommy.
Nola smiled and said, "Yes, this is true."

"The zoo they call Audubon with so much for me to see and do.
Fish, birds, monkeys, and other animals galore.
I really love the zoo mommy, so much I did explore."

"Thanks mommy," Nola said, with her voice loud and clear.
Then mommy simply replied, "Anything for you my dear."

NOLA LOUISE

T.J. Barnes received a Bachelor of Arts in Early Childhood and Elementary Education from the University of New Orleans. She went on to receive a Master's in Educational Leadership from Regent University in Virginia Beach, VA. Barnes resides in Virginia with her son, and human-like poodle. She continues to be passionate about her career as a teacher and educating young children.

Kimmie R. Tubre received a Bachelor of Arts in Communications and Screenwriting from the University of New Orleans. She is currently a free-lance writer for local New Orleans magazines and an occasional blogger. Tubre is also the author of several adult fiction short stories that often take place in her home town, and current place of residence, New Orleans. Both mother and daughter live by the motto, "life without imagination is no life at all."